T0129511

OH, HELL

FUNNY INSIGHTS INTO A STRANGE PLACE WE CALL HELL

T. R. Granville
and
J. L. Ritchie

iUniverse, Inc.
Bloomington

OH, HELL
Funny Insights into a Strange Place We Call Hell

iUniverse books may be ordered through booksellers or by contacting:

iUniverse
1663 Liberty Drive
Bloomington, IN 47403
www.iuniverse.com
1-800-Authors (1-800-288-4677)

ISBN: 978-1-4759-4128-9 (sc)
ISBN: 978-1-4759-4129-6 (ebk)

Library of Congress Control Number: 2012913554

Printed in the United States of America

iUniverse rev. date: 07/28/2012

CONTENTS

To all my family who actually put me through hell several times.

—T. R. Granville

To all my "friends" who drove me to the devil's brew. Guess what? It worked.

—J. L. Ritchie

ACKNOWLEDGMENTS

To all the waiters and waitresses who had to put up with our laughing and carrying on during the writing and spilling of drinks.

To anyone else who may have had a hand in this book that we are not aware of—there aren't any, but we thought we would mention it anyway.

To all the men and women of our armed forces who risk their lives every day to keep us free and safe.

Look for future books from this dynamic duo of breakout authors. Their talent is unlimited and out of control.

Illustrations by Ken Harmon, Denver CO

1

STUFF ABOUT HELL

Hell. What's it all about down there? Some people claim to have been to hell and back. I've heard that story many times. How does that work? If you have really been to hell and back, give some tips to those poor suckers you left behind down there whom you didn't help get the hell out like you did. No wonder you went to hell in the first place—you don't help people.

Next time someone claims to have gone to hell and back, I think we all need to find out how the hell they got out—just in case we know someone who might be going there who does not deserve to go. We hope this book will give us some insight and help us better understand the complexity of that place we call hell.

What to Expect in Hell

- Bowling balls have no holes.
- Deer shoot back.
- Major freeways and expressways have no off ramps.

- Parking garages have all down ramps and no exits.
- Oregano is really just oregano.
- There are no music CDs—just eight-track tapes.
- When you hear voices in your head, it's not your head—it's someone else's.
- The devil is a great dancer because countless people have danced with him.
- If you want to take dance lessons with the devil, there is a very small fee: your soul.

Some people go to hell in a handbasket. Now, that's gotta hurt. I guess that means you have been carved up small enough to fit in a handbasket—not good. The good news is that you can be carried into hell—maybe by one of your friends or the one who actually carved you up in the first place. I am sure some mobsters have gone to hell in a handbasket—even some companies have gone to hell in a handbasket, but it might have been a slightly larger handbasket.

I wonder if there are designer handbaskets. If you happen to be going to hell in small pieces for some reason that I really don't want to know about right now, I think it would be good to go in a designer handbasket. Don't you agree?

I would say a handbasket is probably the worst way for a person to go to hell, but I guess some people don't have a choice in this matter. Someone or something made it possible for you to actually fit in a handbasket—ouch!

What to Expect in Hell

- A full moon means a werewolf is coming to your house for dinner.
- When traveling by car, rest stops are every three thousand miles.
- When a burglar alarm goes off, burglars come within minutes.
- A childproof bottle can be opened only by a child or other little hell-raisers.
- IKEA stores have no arrows on the aisle floors for direction. People roam the store in chaos without knowing which way to go. May heaven help all those poor souls.
- Grocery stores carry only deviled eggs.
- Don't follow breadcrumbs because they only lead to trouble.
- If you see a beanstalk, use common sense. Don't climb it—it won't have a happy ending.

Have you heard the phrase "when hell freezes over"? Not the album by the Eagles rock group—the phrase people use. Now that sounds like one freaking cold front. I love it when I hear a guy say, "I will work for them when hell freezes over." I am guessing he never will, because it would have to be so cold that earth would probably be a snowball. I guess that's when you have a snowball's chance in hell of working somewhere. A snowball's chance in hell—those odds are at least the same odds as winning the lottery. So yes, I am saying you have a chance at winning the lottery, a snowball's chance in hell.

What to Expect in Hell

- Fire hydrants are filled with gasoline.
- The Geek Squad is really just a bunch of geeks with horns.
- Pigs can fly—and not just at airports.
- All the people who live in Florida move north—and all the people in the North move west. Damn it—what the hell? Texas remains the same—thank the devil—even he doesn't want to piss them off.
- Banks and financial firms are always bailed out by the government.
- When your closet door creaks open in the middle of the night, run. I have no idea what it is.
- If you hear noises under your bed in the middle of the night, run faster. It means there must be two creeps in your bedroom.
- Sledding is not a possibility.

2

MORE STUFF ON HELL

I had the pleasure the other day of being pushed aside on the street by a guy rushing by me saying he was "later than hell." What the hell is later than hell? Is it later in hell than it is here? Are the clocks faster there? Are the clocks slower there? How the hell did he even know he was later than hell—unless he's been there? That could be it! He probably has been to hell and back like that other guy. That's why he knows how the clocks work there. He's been to hell and back, and now he's set his wristwatch to hell time. Watch out for those people who have been to hell and back—they are always in a hurry.

Some people say, "This clock is slower than shit." I wonder if the clocks in hell are also slower than shit. Just how slow is shit? That will have to be another book. My brain can't think about all this stuff at once.

What to Expect in Hell

- Water freezes at 1,000 degrees Fahrenheit.
- Bowling alley surfaces are made of sandpaper.

- If Tebow were there, he would still be a saint—and a starting quarterback.
- The loser of the Super Bowl gets a ring of fire and six months of Tebowing lessons.
- *The Simpsons* is on every channel 24/7.
- Every home run in a baseball game hits a spectator in the head when he is returning to his seat with hot dogs and nachos.
- The devil really does wear Prada.

Did you know that Murphy wrote all his laws in hell? I never gave it a thought, but where else could laws that are so diabolical be written? He saw what was going on in hell and wrote some laws for us here on earth. The laws are just devilish enough to aggravate the hell out of us. I guess Murphy's laws are proof there is creativity in hell.

How about hell's kitchen? Some people say, "This kitchen looks like hell." That must be one freaking messed-up kitchen if it looks like hell. I would say some of Murphy's laws probably helped hell's kitchen look like hell.

Buttered toast, when accidentally dropped, always lands buttered side first. Also, Ramen noodles are very popular in hell's kitchen because half the noodles go all over the kitchen when you open the package.

Hell's kitchen is a great place to run when hell freezes over because of all the grease fires that will be burning and the devil's brew that will be boiling. It should be warm and fuzzy.

And who the hell is Murphy anyway—and why is he writing laws? Is he some "damned-to-hell-forever" attorney that just won't give up? Maybe he was the first person who went to hell and back. Maybe he was the first attorney to be damned to hell. He probably set up a nice practice there for himself. He's working day and night, popping out all those crazy laws that just drive us nuts.

He loves it down there in hell and feels his laws are payback for all the attorney jokes we tell here on earth.

What to Expect in Hell

- Baby alligators put their heads in small children's mouths.
- All stop signs say GO.
- All the arrows at an intersection turn green at the same time.
- Democrats are in charge.
- Cars have gas mileage of one mile per tank.
- Gas stations are every two miles.
- Gas pumps also dispense cigarettes and matches.
- Tattoos are not put on—they are ripped off.

Have you ever been around the office when the boss comes back from vacation? He usually asks the secretary, "How's it been around here while I was gone?"

The secretary will most times say, "It's been hell around here."

The boss might say, "Oh really? I did not notice your flesh—or anyone else's around here—melting off the bone. I don't see anyone's hair on fire or pitchforks sticking out of their butts. Doesn't look like hell to me."

He must be one of the guys who has been to hell and back. He knows what he's looking for.

What to Expect in Hell

- Alcohol is available for adults as Step 13 of Alcoholics Anonymous.
- Marijuana is available only by prescription and for medical purposes. Wow! That's major.
- The ending of a movie is revealed at the beginning of the movie.
- Attorneys are still attorneys. I guess some things never change.
- Everyone who said he or she would see you in hell isn't there.
- Chinese buffets are just as good.
- A raffle is always won by the raffle organizer.
- Skateboarders are forced to perform their stunts over open shark tanks.
- Sharks think they are surfers. Therefore, it works well—everybody's happy.

3

A LITTLE BIT
MORE ON HELL

"How the hell did that happen?" I love that phrase. I guess it happened the same way it happens in hell. I don't know. The fact that it happened at all is amazing. I would guess it happens that way in hell because where else would it happen that way? I guess we could consult our handy guide—*How the Hell Things Happen in Hell*—to find the answers. How the hell do I know? I don't know it all. I haven't been to hell and back yet. When I do go to hell and back, I will let you know how the hell it happened.

What to Expect in Hell

- The only doctor available is a proctologist—and he doesn't wear gloves.
- The doctor says, "That's one hell of a rash." The patient responds, "Is there an app for that?"
- The Tooth Fairy is a dental hygienist—apparently experience pays.

- Your surgeon is an alcoholic and a chain smoker. To top that off, he has a bad case of Parkinson's disease but has good crypt-side manner.
- At Halloween, children wear Jesus costumes.
- The game of golf consists of 118 holes of pure hell. It's the same as on earth—just 100 holes longer.
- Par for a round of golf is 666 for the full 118 holes.
- Fairways are sand, and the sand traps are grass.

"Hey, you're going to go to hell for that." Is there a list of things not to do? If so, let's get an iPhone application to help us. How do the people who say that really know unless they have already been to hell and back—and brought back a list of things that could send you to hell? What the hell—I guess we will take our chances. Most of us have probably already burned through that list anyway.

What to Expect in Hell

- Disneyland's PA system at each ride is still unintelligible except for the parting words: "Thank you for riding."
- At Disneyland's Haunted Mansion, you are the ghost.
- "It's a Small World" is the theme song as you enter the gates of hell.
- Disneyland's Carousel of Progress shows no progress at all.
- Disneyland's Future World ride is your life in hell.

- Hiking trails are always uphill and infested with rattlesnakes and malaria-carrying mosquitoes. If you wanted downhill trails and no hazards, you should have gone to heaven.
- Hell actually freezes over at 4,000 degrees Fahrenheit.
- iPods play only rap music and "The Devil Went down to Georgia."

4

A HELL OF A BIT MORE STUFF

"What the devil is that?" What does that mean? Whatever it is, it can't be good. Whatever it is, the devil had something to do with it—and that can't be a good thing.

"Who the devil are you?" "What the devil's in my cereal?" "Where the devil are my slippers?" These expressions are all said every day—I would bet mostly by an older generation of folks. I love the first one. My mother used to say that to me all the time. I guess she forgot who I was—or my room was too messy.

I think we need to consult the *What, Who, and Where the Devil Everything Is Guidebook* to figure all that out. Or we could consult someone who has been to hell and back.

What to Expect in Hell

- Men and women are actually from the same planet.
- The coffee isn't cold at all—it is 9,000 degrees Fahrenheit.

- Family photos always include a photo of O. J. Simpson.
- Everyone makes calls to telemarketers during dinnertime.
- There is always a line at the men's room only.
- In football, the third-string quarterback is also the head of the cheerleading squad.
- The animal pictures on an unmentioned airline's plane tail are actual photos of your pilot.
- Flight attendants are not just glorified waitresses—thank God.
- Smoke detectors are always going off.
- A fire hazard is a good thing.

"I hope you rot in hell." That's a good one people say. If there was something else they could be doing down there besides rotting, I think they'd be doing it. I would say rotting is probably not much fun—but, then again, it is hell. Do the people who say that to other people really mean it? Saying that could be on the list of things that send you to hell.

I can see it now—a line of people waiting at the gates of hell. A demon with a pen and pad of paper says, "Folks, listen up. Anyone who was told by someone on earth that they hoped you would rot in hell, please step to your left. You will be rotting in hell. Everyone else, step to your right. You will be rotting in hell also. That's all we do here. Sorry. But thank you for forming two lines for rotting—it makes it quicker for processing. Anyone carrying a handbasket, please move to the front of the line and put the handbaskets on the tables. Folks, this is your first meal here in hell. We will try to make your stay here as uncomfortable as possible."

What to Expect in Hell

- Politicians are still politicians
- Drawing a line in the sand must mean there is no paper.
- Man's best friend is his serpent.
- There are no Budweiser commercials during the Super Bowl. Damn—this really is hell.
- Monkeys can fly.
- Scarecrows are living beings.
- Children are given black permanent markers and told to "go for it."
- When told, children really do go play in traffic.
- You have to report all the things you said the devil made you do—to see if they are really true. It's called accountability, my friend.

"I will see you in hell." I know you have heard this phrase—but it's not always directed at you, of course. If someone says it, I guess both of you are going to hell. If that's the case, it might be easier if one of the two parties is going to hell in a handbasket.

I would have to believe that a lot of shootouts and fights are started by someone saying, "I will see you in hell." Most times, this is followed by the phrase: "You first!" When you hear that, you know someone may be going to hell in a handbasket.

Sometimes, you may hear the following exchange in an argument between two parties:

Party One says, "See you in hell."

Party Two responds, "You first."

Party One says, "No—you first."

That is when all hell breaks loose. I know we have not even discussed all hell breaking loose yet, but it usually happens when the right words are spoken in the correct order as you just have read them.

You do not want to be around when all hell is breaking loose. All hell breaking loose means that hell has come to earth for that short period of time—and you do not want to be around when that happens. There will be some folks going to hell during the hell-breaking-loose period—and you don't want to be mistaken for one of those people. Many times, handbaskets are needed for some of the participating parties. Hell has been known to come to earth for longer breaking-loose periods, such as wars and plagues.

Either way, when all hell breaks loose, get the hell out of the way.

What to Expect in Hell

- Cowardly lions are not allowed.
- The Wicked Witch of the West is a mild-mannered librarian.
- The Wicked Witch of the East turned back and said it wasn't nasty enough.
- Laundry detergent does not remove bloodstains from shirts.
- Bloodstained shirts are very common.
- ATM machines dispense money and the phone numbers of well-known Ponzi scheme financial planners to invest it with.
- Your car has four tires, but they are not on your vehicle. They are in the back of a pickup truck heading to the hood. Not to worry, you still have

your stinking hubcaps. Those of you with custom rims can "forget about it."

"It's been a hell of a long time." How in the hell does anyone know how much is a long time in hell? I would say any time spent in hell would be a long time for sure. Some folks say, "It's been a hell of a long time since we have seen each other."

Maybe he has been to hell and back—I am not sure. But if he is always running late, maybe it's true. Maybe he is later than hell because his watch is set to hell time—which is late. If any of this makes sense to you, I would be surprised because it's been a hell of a long time since I started this book. Where the devil it's going, I don't know.

What to Expect in Hell

- Men's hair gel is highly flammable.
- Men's baldness is a good thing.
- Turtles are the fastest creatures.
- They use hot sauce as an antacid.
- Casper the Friendly Ghost is not so friendly.
- You can tell a redneck by his red neck and possibly his red tail.
- Bicycles are basically the same—except the chain is around your neck and the pump is who knows where. Take a guess.

5

WOW! THERE'S STILL MORE STUFF

"It's the devil's brew." Have you heard this? How about a little recipe? What the hell is the devil brewing—and why is he brewing it? How does anyone know it's the devil's brew anyway? Oh, I forgot—the guy who has been to hell and back knows what the devil's brew is.

My guess is that it would be my ex-wife's cooking. Sometimes at dinner, I say, "What the hell is this?" Hence, she is now "The Ex."

I have had some beer over the years—that might qualify as the devil's brew.

Sun Screen

SPF 500

For Those
in HELL ONLY

Also Delays
Rotting

What to Expect in Hell

- Cigarette machines dispense nails as well as coffins.
- Sunscreen is 500 SPF on average.
- Cell phone reception is exactly the same—terrible.
- Cell phone batteries last two minutes. Who are you calling anyway?
- Having botulism is a good day.
- Everyone lives in a cul-de-sac, and the other homeowners are the Munsters, the Addams Family, Norman Bates, and the Cleavers.

"The devil made me do it." Now there's a good one. Like the devil has the time to make you do things. He's got hell to maintain—and I am sure that takes a lot of his time. He has hell breaking loose at different times all over the world and people lining up at the gates of hell—some in handbaskets.

The devil has a major business to run here. I don't know if he is making small children write on walls with black permanent markers. Now, if a child writes "Redrum" on a wall in blood, that's a different story. You better get the hell out of there because all hell could be breaking loose very shortly.

"The devil made me do it!" Yeah right, I don't think so—you're just an ass. I love it when these same people say they hear voices telling them to do terrible things. After all is said and done, the only voice they are going to hear in the night is from Bobby Joe in the upper bunk telling him how much he loves him. That's called paying the devil his due.

What to Expect in Hell

- Hitler runs a soup kitchen—a true soup Nazi.
- Hitler and Napoleon are both still trying to mount comebacks.
- The fire department works 24/7 without pay in a building made of dried wood chips.
- Every morning, your hair dryer breaks down after setting your hair on fire.
- Your locker combination is always 666—and you always forget it when you come back from vacation.
- Firemen are really just men on fire.
- Vacations are at the nearest hot spot, which is usually a volcano.
- The devil drives a 1972 Firebird, and everyone else drives a 1972 Gremlin or Pinto—your choice.
- Whatever you drive, remember the Pinto might explode on rear impact. Be safe.
- The Elephant Man is considered handsome.
- A man with George Clooney's looks would be turned away for fear of scaring the other doomed souls.
- There is no soda pop taste challenge, but there is the embalming fluid versus battery acid challenge.

"That was a hell of a good time." How the hell could hell and a good time be connected? If you're having a good time in hell, you really must have been a bad person on earth. Hell apparently is a good place for those monstrous people. Hell must be a mild place for them—possibly a step up. I wonder if they send letters back from hell.

Hi Dear,

I am having a great time here in hell—lots of partying and hell-raising. I met an old friend of mine the other day. When I shook his hand, his arm fell off. He's been here a while, I think. It sounds like a rotting issue to me. I have to say I am having a great time and living with you must have really been hell because I am actually happy again. Got to go now—a flaming lawn jart game is about to start. I am the team captain.

PS Took a flaming lawn jart in the head the other day—and I am still happier here.

What to Expect in Hell

- Elevators only go down.
- You can try a rain dance, but it won't work.
- The most interesting man in the world isn't very interesting anymore.
- A hot iron has a double meaning and purpose.
- The Nazi War Machine is a popular rock group.
- The Hatfields and McCoys love each other.
- The *Psycho* house is a popular rest stop.
- *Psycho* is considered a good old-fashioned love story.
- Peanut butter and jelly-fish sandwiches are very popular
- Snakes are snakes, and spiders are spiders—and I am still scared of both.

Hellcat

When I was a kid, we had a cat from hell. Shadow was a black Siamese cat. He ruled our home for twelve years. Shadow terrorized my mother, my sister, and me. The cat somehow thought that it owned our home—and we were squatters that were interfering with his life as a cat.

I learned very quickly not to reach into my dark closet at night. If that devil cat was in there, he would rip my wrists open with his claws. We were scared most of the time—not knowing where he was hiding or when would he pounce on us. We could always tell where and when someone discovered him by the screams and occasional tears that followed. My mother and sister bore the brunt of Shadow's cruelty and possessed behavior. I usually locked my bedroom door at night and held my bodily functions until the morning light so I would not die at an early age.

My father had a very simple way of handling the situation. Upon seeing the cat, he would grab it. Shadow never expected it because he was used to people running away from him. My father would open the front door and heave Shadow into the nearest snowdrift, curse a few words, and slam the door.

Shadow must have had his own key to the house. We would never let him back inside—especially if the kids where home alone. When we moved out of that house, the cat stayed. From what I heard from the neighbors, the hellcat sold the home several years later. So, yes, I really believe it was his house.

What to Expect in Hell

- Freddy Krueger is a well-liked pediatrician.
- You can kill two birds with one brimstone.
- Lightning does strike twice—if you're lucky. Of course, to increase your odds, stand under a tree.
- Railroad crossings are a trap. Once you start across the tracks, both railroad crossing arms come down.
- At Wimbledon, the grass is six inches long. Players are given a tennis racquet and grass clippers.
- The French Open is played on a wet clay surface. Players are given a tennis racquet and a squeegee.
- The French love the English, but they still hate Americans.

Dancing with the Devil

A while ago, at a restaurant, I ran into a friend I had not seen for some time.

He said, "Where the hell have you been—dancing with the devil?"

I said, "No, I haven't. First of all, I don't dance. Secondly, I did not even know the devil gave dance lessons. Thirdly, I have been trying to avoid the devil all my life. Why in the world would I seek him out to get dance lessons? And, fourthly, how do you even know the devil can dance or even give lessons?"

When I realized my friend must have been to hell and back, I asked to see his wonderful wristwatch.

He said, "Why do you want to see my watch?"

"I just want to check the time."

When he showed me the time, I realized his wristwatch was not running on hell time—it was just slower than shit. I was relieved that my friend had not been to hell and back—and it was just a slow-as-shit watch he was wearing.

Some people do dance with the devil; usually it's their last dance—period.

6

MORE HELL TO
CONTEND WITH

We came across some interesting places in the world with strange names. We are definitely not going to check out any of these places ourselves; we will have to leave that up to the readers since they are too strange for even us.

Places like the following

Hell Station, Hell, Norway
Hell Creek, Montana
Hell, Michigan
Bloody Corners, Ohio
Devil's Backbone, Connecticut
Devil's Den, Wyoming
Devil's Elbow, California
Devil Town, Ohio
Devils Tower, Wyoming
Half Hell, North Carolina
Hell for Certain, Kentucky
Kill Devil Hills, North Carolina

Red Devil, Alaska
Slaughter Beach, Delaware
Skullhead, Georgia
Slaughterville, Oklahoma
Spook City, Colorado
Tombstone, Arizona
Transylvania, Louisiana
Witch Lake, Michigan
Bloody Pond Road, Lake George, New York
Psycho Path, Michigan
Purgatory Road, Texas
Bucket of Blood Street, Arizona
Grave's End Neck Road, New York
Sleepy Hollow Road, Pennsylvania
Shades of Death Road, New Jersey
Route 666, Somewhere
Half Hell, North Carolina (This must be a bad place, but I guess it's not quite hellish enough for the full hell.)
Kill Devil Hills, North Carolina (This sounds like a nice subdivision.)

Wow! Can you believe some of the strange names of towns and roads? Imagine having a party for friends and coworkers and living in one of these places. If I was giving directions to my house, it might go something like this:

Drive to Bloody Corners, Ohio, and take a right on Purgatory Road. Go one mile and turn left on Bloody Pond Road. Follow that until it turns into Bucket of Blood Street. Follow that street to Psycho Path and turn right on Graves End Neck Road. I am the thirteenth house on the left, number 666. If you get to Shades of

Death Road, you have gone too far. If you do get to Shades of Death Road, you have approximately sixty seconds to get out of there—there is a reason for the name.

Hope you can make it.
PS Bring a dish to pass.

To Hell You'll Ride!

I don't know about you, but if someone offers me a ride to hell, I am walking there for sure. Why would anyone want to get there faster? I will walk there, thank you. Maybe I will get run over while I am walking and won't have to go. Maybe if you die twice on the way to hell, you don't have to go. Maybe—just maybe—if you get lost on the way, the demons won't be able to find you and drag you to the gates of hell.

It's worth the shot not to go—don't you think? It is like trying to get out of jury duty or something. I am trying to come up with all kinds of excuses for not going and not showing up at those gates.

If the devil were smart, he would make the gates look very nice and put up false signage: "Pearl gates, welcome, cold ice tea ahead." Some people would be suckered in—there is a sucker born every minute.

Hell Tours, Inc.

Take a tour of hell and get a look at what hell has to offer. You might see some old friends or enemies on your tour.

Tours start out from New York on the SS *Titanic*; this obviously is not her maiden voyage. Her maiden voyage did not go so well and, therefore, made this ship available for our hell tours. There will be plenty of ice for your drinks—don't worry.

The trip will head down to the Bermuda Triangle off the Florida coast and then disappear. We hope it will reappear in hell.

Attire for your tour should be bloodstained shirts, shorts, and sandals. If you do not have bloodstained attire, don't worry. We can make them bloodstained for you before boarding.

We have a dentist who used to be a butcher on staff. Rotten teeth will be removed at no charge.

Rules for the Hell Tour

- Flash photography is not allowed.
- Flashing is allowed.
- No children under six years of age.
- If arriving with children under the age of six, they will be served as dinner later.
- You can bring a family member for an intervention. They will be subjected to more hell than the rest you—we hope that will set them straight.
- No recording devices allowed—it would just sound like screaming anyway. Why bother?
- The tour will make three bathroom breaks and twenty vomit breaks. If you need more than twenty vomit breaks, you probably should have not eaten so much at lunch.

- Please leave your business card in our raffle bucket upon boarding.
- One of you will not return from hell—and that will be the winner of the raffle.
- The ship leaves at midnight on Friday the Thirteenth of every month only.
- If you have a pacemaker, don't worry, we will remove it upon boarding.
- If you have any other serious medical conditions, save your money. Do not take this tour. You will probably be dying soon and might be going to hell for free.
- If you have a fear of hot-as-hell branding irons or can't stand the smell of burning flesh, you may want to change your vacation plans.
- If you have sensitive skin, the branding iron might irritate it further. Please change your travel plans.
- Tour costs are $666.00 and an extra $6.66 to see the devil's crib.

7

OH, HELL! THE END!

The devil had nothing to do with us writing this book. It came very naturally, and with the help of the devil's brew, it became much clearer and easier to write. We hope to see you in heaven. If not, see you in hell—and don't forget to set your watches to hell time so you are not running later than hell.

The End (Maybe)

Printed in the United States
By Bookmasters